LITTLE BIG BOOK PLUS

Table of Contents

Meet
Mirra Ginsburg

When she was growing up, Mirra Ginsburg's parents taught her to love books. Now she likes to write her own!

Meet
Jose Aruego and
Ariane Dewey

Jose Aruego likes to draw animals. He says, "It seems no matter how I draw them, they look funny." Ariane Dewey added the color to Mr. Aruego's drawings.

The Chick
and the Duckling

Translated from the Russian of V. Suteyev

by Mirra Ginsburg
Pictures by Jose Aruego & Ariane Dewey

HOUGHTON MIFFLIN COMPANY
BOSTON
ATLANTA   DALLAS   GENEVA, ILLINOIS   PALO ALTO   PRINCETON

Acknowledgments

For each of the selections listed below, grateful acknowledgment is made for permission to excerpt and/or reprint original or copyrighted material, as follows:

Text

1 *The Chick and the Duckling,* by Mirra Ginsburg, illustrated by Jose Aruego and Ariane Dewey. Copyright © 1972 by Mirra Ginsburg. Illustrations copyright © 1972 by Jose Aruego. Reprinted by permission of Macmillan Books for Young Readers, Simon & Schuster Children's Publishing Division. **33** "Big," from *All Together,* by Dorothy Aldis. Copyright © 1925–1928, 1934, 1939, 1952, copyright renewed 1953–1956, 1962, 1967 by Dorothy Aldis. Reprinted by permission of G.P. Putnam's Sons. **37** "A Duckling Grows Up," from January 1995 *Your Big Backyard* magazine. Copyright © 1980 by the National Wildlife Federation. Reprinted by permission. **38** "I'm a yellow-bill duck," from *Ride a Purple Pelican,* by Jack Prelutsky. Copyright © 1986 by Jack Prelutsky. Reprinted by permission of Greenwillow Books, a division of William Morrow & Company, Inc.

Illustrations

34–36 Juan Carlos Nichols.

Photography

i Tim Davis/Tony Stone Images (tl, bl, br); Nino Mascardi/The Image Bank (tr). **ii** Courtesy of Mirra Ginsburg (tr); George Schiavone/The Stock Market (cl); Nino Mascardi/The Image Bank (cr); Michal Heron (bl). **37** Breck P. Kent (cover); Jack Dermid (tr); Stephen J. Krasemann/DRK Photo (bl). **38** Mike Mazzaschi/Stock Boston (tl); Willard Traub (b).

Houghton Mifflin Edition, 1999
Copyright © 1999 by Houghton Mifflin Company. All rights reserved.

Printed in the U.S.A.

ISBN 0-395-91660-7

123456789-B-04 03 02 01 00 99 98

to Libby

A Duckling came out
of the shell.

"I am out!" he said.

"Me too," said the Chick.

"I am taking a walk,"
said the Duckling.

"Me too,"
said the Chick.

"I am digging a hole,"
said the Duckling.

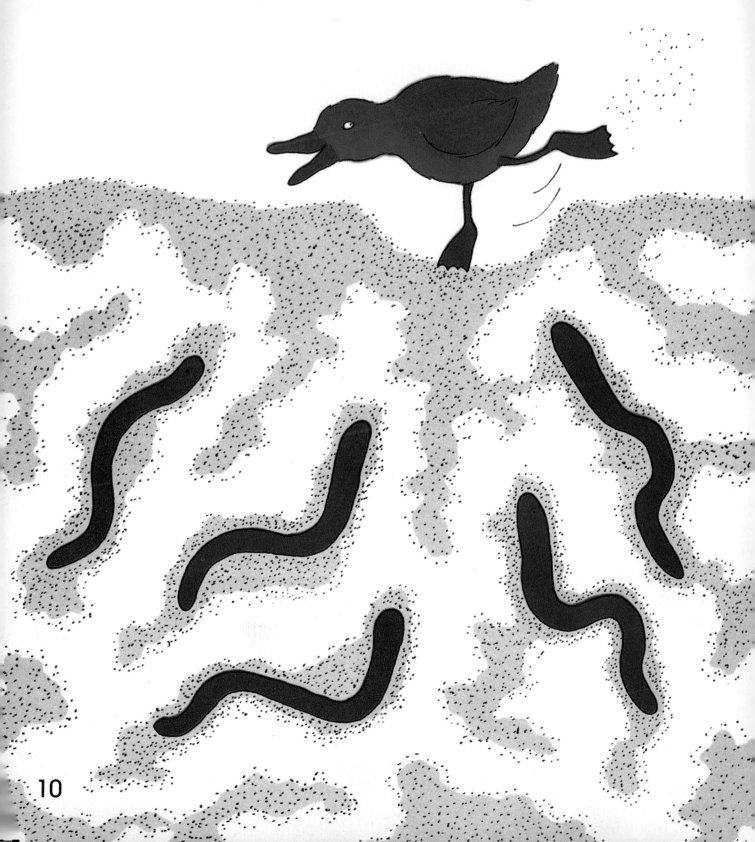

11

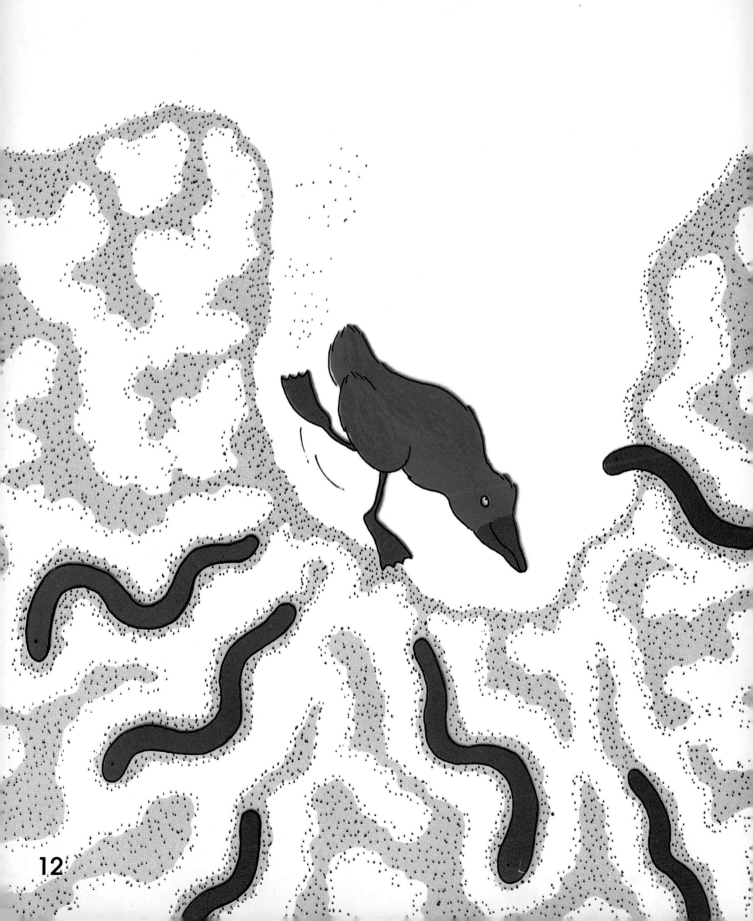

"Me too,"
said the Chick.

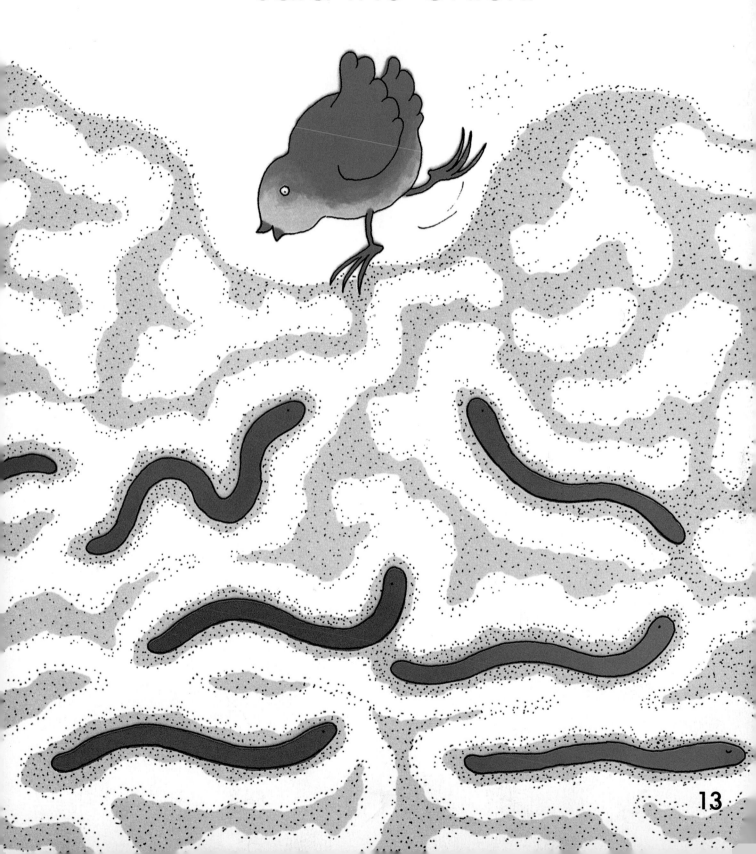

"I found a worm,"
said the Duckling.

"Me too,"
said the Chick.

"I caught
a butterfly,"
said the
Duckling.

"Me too,"
said the Chick.

19

"I am going for a swim,"
said the Duckling.

"Me too,"
  said the Chick.

"I am swimming,"
said the Duckling.

"Me too!"
cried the Chick.

The Duckling pulled the Chick out.

"I'm going for another swim,"
said the Duckling.

"Not me,"
said the Chick.

BIG

Now I can catch and throw a ball

And spell

Cat. Dog.

And Pig,

I have finished being small

And started

Being Big.

by Dorothy Aldis

Los pollitos dicen

una canción tradicional

Los pollitos dicen:
–pío, pío, pío
–cuando tienen hambre,
cuando tienen frío.

The Baby Chicks Sing

a traditional song

The baby chicks are saying,
"Peep, peep, peep,"
Because they're cold and hungry;
Because they need some sleep.

34

La gallina busca
el maíz y el trigo;
les da de comer,
y les presta abrigo.

The hen brings her little chicks
Brown wheat and yellow corn.
She feeds them all their dinner,
And makes sure they stay warm.

Bajo sus dos alas,
acurrucaditos,
hasta el otro día
duermen los pollitos.

Underneath her two wings
Their mother hugs them tight,
So the baby chicks can sleep
All through the frosty night.

A **Duckling** Grows Up

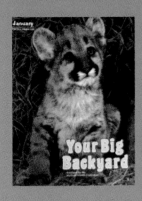

This is what a wood duck looks like when it is about one day old.

This is a male wood duck. He is all grown up.

I'm a **Yellow-Bill** Duck

by Jack Prelutsky

I'm a yellow-bill duck
with a black feather back,
I waddle waddle waddle,
and I **quack quack quack!**

I dabble for my dinner
with a swish swish swish,
and I gobble gobble gobble
all I wish wish wish!

Make Way for Ducklings, sculpture by Nancy Schön
Boston, Massachusetts